Snugglepot *and* Cuddlepie go home

Retold by Anna Fienberg
Illustrated by Vicky Kitanov

Angus&Robertson
An imprint of HarperCollins*Publishers*

Angus&Robertson
An imprint of HarperCollins*Publishers*, Australia

First published in 1997
by HarperCollins*Publishers* Pty Limited
ACN 009 913 517
A member of the HarperCollins*Publishers* (Australia) Pty Limited Group

Copyright text and illustration © The Spastic Centre of New South Wales and The Northcott Society, 1997

This book is copyright.
Apart from any fair dealing for the purposes of private study, research,
criticism or review, as permitted under the Copyright Act, no part may
be reproduced by any process without written permission.
Inquiries should be addressed to the publishers.

HarperCollins*Publishers*
25 Ryde Road, Pymble, Sydney, NSW 2073, Australia
31 View Road, Glenfield, Auckland 10, New Zealand
77–85 Fulham Palace Road, London W6 8JB, United Kingdom
Hazelton Lanes, 55 Avenue Road, Suite 2900, Toronto, Ontario M5R 3L2
and 1995 Markham Road, Scarborough, Ontario M1B 5M8, Canada
10 East 53rd Street, New York NY 10032, USA

National Library of Australia Cataloguing-in-Publication data:

Fienberg, Anna.
The world of May Gibbs.
ISBN 0 207 19118 2 (6).
I. Gibbs, May, 1877-1969. Complete adventures of Snugglepot and Cuddlepie. II. Kitanov, Vicky.
III. Title. IV. Title: Complete adventures of Snugglepot and Cuddlepie.
A823.2

Printed in Hong Kong
9 8 7 6 5 4 3 2 1   97 98 99

The World of May Gibbs

Here are the adventures of Snugglepot and Cuddlepie. They were Gumnut babies, almost brothers. This is how it came about.

When Cuddlepie was just a few hours old, a great wind arose and lifted him out of his mother's arms. The wind carried him far away, over tree-tops and hills, until it dropped him in a spider web. Luckily, a kind Nut saw him fall, and gently carried poor Cuddlepie home.

Now this was the home of Snugglepot, and the kind Nut brought them up side by side as brothers, happy and strong.

Now, would you like to hear some secrets of the sea? We can dive down, below the boats and the gulls and the sun that spreads like honey on the waves. Let's go down under, where there are dark places and light places, to where the Fish Folk live.

Down there, you'll find roads winding through forests of sea-trees and strange anemones growing amongst the coral. But in the dark caves, at the bottom of the sea, giant monsters live. Some have long lashing tentacles, others are as tall as mountains.

We know all this because once, two brave little Gumnuts - Snugglepot and Cuddlepie - ventured down, under the sea.

The Gumnuts' home was in the Bush but they were adventurers and often went to stay with the Fish Folk beneath the waves. Ann Chovy was a friend of theirs and there was always room for them in her house.

Ann gave them little shell-beds to sleep in; they ate sea grapes for breakfast and prawns for tea. One day they took Ann's sea horses for a ride and strayed a little too far. That was when they saw the cave and the giant monsters.

Well, early one morning Cuddlepie was sitting at breakfast, tasting some fish eggs for a change. He was remembering a dream he'd had - a dream of the Giant Octopus who had once nearly eaten them all up - when Snugglepot burst in. 'Sting and wing me!' he cried, flinging himself down at the table. 'Let's go and see something new today!'

Cuddlepie choked on his eggs. This was exactly how the day of the Giant Octopus had begun. Snugglepot was always wanting to go exploring. Sometimes, on these adventures, the Gumnuts made wonderful new friends like Mr Lizard who lived in the Bush - but sometimes they had to run for their lives.

Cuddlepie didn't feel like running. His heart started to pound just at the thought of it. He'd been looking forward to a nice quiet day wandering in the garden and perhaps meeting the children after Fish Folk School.

'And we haven't seen Ragged Blossom since yesterday,' said Cuddlepie. 'She could come over and play.'

Ragged Blossom, the Gumnuts' best friend, had gone to sea with them.

Now she lived with the wise and beautiful sea princess, Obelia, whom she had found when the little princess was just a baby in a pearl shell.

'You know how Ragged Blossom likes to visit our garden,' Cuddlepie went on. 'And we can play hide-and-seek with the flowers.'

Snugglepot nodded, for sea flowers don't grow in the ground like land flowers - they get up and walk about!

'All right, let's go and pick up Ragged Blossom,' said Snugglepot. 'And maybe we can teach her the rules today.'

Ragged Blossom loved to play hide-and-seek, but she needed a lot of practice with the 'hiding' part. When it was her turn to hide, she became so fidgety and nervous, all alone, that she couldn't wait to be found and always burst out too early, calling 'Here I am! Find me, quick!'

Well, the Nuts finished their breakfast and went out to the stables to saddle up the sea horses.

But isn't it strange - sometimes even when you decide you won't go out looking for adventure, it comes to you, right over the garden wall, right into your home! (This is especially likely to happen if you live under the sea.)

The Gumnuts had just arrived back home with Ragged Blossom and they were about to begin a game when a great fish came rushing over the wall, his dark nose shining and his eyes glistening. Swift and straight he darted at the children and before they could even cry out he had opened his huge jaws and swallowed them up. Then with a swish of his tail he turned and rushed away into the dark forest of sea-trees.

It seemed a long, long time to the Gumnuts and Ragged Blossom. They crouched in the gurgling blackness, barely breathing. But it couldn't have been more than a few moments, because almost immediately after the greedy fish swallowed them, he spied the bait on the end of a young boy's fishing line and snapped it up.

'Got him!' shouted the boy, whose name was Billy.
'Haul him in,' said his father.
'A beauty,' chuckled Billy, as he swung the fish into the boat.

'He'll do nicely,' said Billy's father, taking out his knife. 'I'll prepare him while you row in.' Suddenly he sprang up. 'Will you look at that!' he exclaimed.

'What?' cried Billy, craning forward. 'Oh, Dad!' he gasped in amazement. 'What can it be? How wonderful!'

For there, in the middle of the opened fish, sat three little creatures. Snugglepot, Cuddlepie and Ragged Blossom. While Billy and his father stared with eyes and mouth wide open in astonishment, the little Nuts and Blossom jumped out and ran along the side of the boat.

'Catch 'em! Quick, Dad! Catch 'em!' shouted Billy.

The father lurched about, rocking the boat dangerously. The boy kept shouting out 'There! There!' and pointing wildly in every direction.

Just then Snugglepot spied a coil of rope lying tucked up near the bow.

'Follow me!' he called to the others, and he raced toward the rope and flung himself into it, wriggling underneath like a beetle. Cuddlepie and Ragged Blossom slid under too just as the Humans came stomping up with their great feet.

'Where did they go?' cried Billy. 'Oh, I can't see them anywhere - we've lost them!'

There was silence in the boat. The only sound was the soft slapping of the water against its sides. The Gumnuts held their breath.

'This is just like hide-and-seek,' whispered Cuddlepie. He was starting to giggle he was so nervous.

'*Sh!*' said Snugglepot. But it was too late. Ragged

Blossom had heard. She began to fidget under the rope. She scratched her nose and wriggled her shoulders. She sighed and crossed her toes with anxiety. Finally she couldn't wait any longer. She pushed up an inch of rope and burst out, calling 'Here I am! Find me, quick!'

'There!' cried Billy, swinging about. 'Near the rope!'

Snugglepot and Cuddlepie dashed out and ran along the side of the boat after Ragged Blossom. Suddenly fingers as long as snakes closed around their chests and they felt as if the breath was being squeezed right out of them as they dangled way up there in the sky.

'Fill the specimen bottle and we'll put them in,' said the father as he peered at the remarkable little creatures he held in his hands. Billy brought the bottle; and without waiting for lunch he and his father hurried home to show everyone their wonderful find.

Ragged Blossom clung to the Gumnuts in the bottle as the Humans stared at them. Every now and then the big people shook the bottle to make them move and their poor little heads were quite sore with being bumped against the sides.

'Just because we are little they think we can't feel,' said Cuddlepie, glaring fiercely at the huge face of Billy, who simply did not know any better. At last, night came and the Humans all went to bed.

'I hate Humans!' said poor Cuddlepie, pushing at the heavy lid. It was stuck fast and they might as well have tried to push back a mountain.

Eventually they drifted off to sleep exhausted by all the terrors of the day.

They never knew it, our three young friends from the Bush, but a little while later Billy crept in with his torch. He pointed it to the side of the bottle, so that the heart of the shining circle just missed the sleeping Gumnuts - only its soft outline lit up their faces.

He stayed there, resting his chin on his hand, for a long time. He watched the way the creatures sighed in their sleep. He saw how they cuddled up to each other. Billy's eyes filled with tears. He wished he could know these creatures better. But he also knew, deep in his heart, what he had to do.

Very gently, he grasped the bottle and loosened the lid. He shone the torch again for one last look and walked out of the room.

The moon rose and a soft breeze tugged at the curtain. Some time later, just near birdrise, an owl flew by the window, hooting loudly. Snugglepot woke up, startled, and tried again to push at the lid. This time it just fell off, like a loose button!

There was a clang and the others woke with a start.

'How did you do that?' cried Cuddlepie, giving his brother a hug.

Ragged Blossom gasped with joy.

'Scrub and rub me,' Snugglepot shrugged happily, 'my Gumnut muscles must be growing. Come on, let's get out of here!'

Cuddlepie and Ragged Blossom followed Snugglepot, clambering out of the bottle and falling on top of each other. They slid along the tablecloth, ran along the floor, climbed up the window curtain and in a moment were out on the sill of the open window.

The moon was shining. It lay like a great silver pool over the grass. The trees rustled in the breeze and the smell of earth and gum leaves perfumed the air. Snugglepot, Cuddlepie and Ragged Blossom took great deep breaths, glad, just for now, to be back on dry ground.

'Sh! . . . Sh! . . . Sh!' It was the voice of a possum walking along the bough of a gum tree growing close beside the house.

'Mr Possum!' called Cuddlepie, trembling in case the Humans should hear him.

'Hello!' called back Mr Possum, lowering himself by his tail to see who it was.

'Take us into the tree,' cried Ragged Blossom. 'We're so frightened the Humans will catch us. Oh, quick!'

Reaching out his hands, Mr Possum swung them all up into the tree and took them safely to his little house in the Bush nearby. By this time Ragged Blossom was so worn out and overwhelmed by all the frights that she had suffered that she fell upon Mrs Possum's motherly breast and wept.

'If-if only dear Mr Lizard would come and take us home,' she sobbed.

Cuddlepie patted her shoulder. 'Wouldn't it be gummy,' he agreed. 'Wouldn't it be the best thing in the whole world to see our dear old friend's face right now?'

Now the strangest of strange things happened. The door opened and who do you think walked in? Mr Lizard! It was just as if this was the theatre, thought Cuddlepie, and their friend had been waiting behind the curtains to play his part.

'Stump and bump me!' cried Mr Lizard, 'if it isn't my dearest little friends! I thought you were down under with the Fish Folk. Tell me, how did you ever come to be here·in Mr Possum's house?'

When Mr and Mrs Possum saw all their visitors throwing their arms about each other's necks and talking and laughing and dancing about, they held up their hands in surprise.

'Let's get something to eat and drink – let's celebrate!' cried Mr Possum, and he and his wife brought out some nice cold aphis milk for everyone.

And so Snugglepot began telling tales of the sea and there was so much to say and so much to explain, that the sun had risen high in the sky and the birds were singing by the time they had finished.

'Come on then,' said Mr Lizard, yawning and stretching his legs. 'I'll give you all a lift to Gumnut Town.'

And after they had thanked Mr and Mrs Possum, Snugglepot, Cuddlepie and Ragged Blossom hopped onto Mr Lizard's back and began the long journey home.

All the Nuts and Blossoms in Gumnut Town crowded around to see them and they had great celebrations. Then, as Snugglepot announced, it was time to make plans . . .

Well, the Gumnuts didn't feel like any more adventures under the sea for a while. Snugglepot decided to build a new, big house and he took Cuddlepie and Ragged Blossom to live with him! Mr Lizard went off scouring the countryside for another friend of theirs from the Bush, Winky Jerboa. He found Winky lost and nearly starving. He brought him to Snugglepot who was so happy to see him that he asked Winky to be head

gardener and live with him always. Little Winky stuffed his tail into his mouth to hide his tears – he was so happy.

Yet Ragged Blossom missed her baby Obelia. Her wise little sea princess.

'But she's not a baby now: she's grown up,' said Cuddlepie.

'But I'd *like* a baby,' said Ragged Blossom.

'Well, sting and wing me!' cried Snugglepot. 'You shall have one. You can have as many as you like. We could gather up all the little homeless Bush babies and start a Gumnut nursery. I'll build it next door to our new house.'

'And Mr Lizard can design an adventure playground!' suggested Cuddlepie.

Ragged Blossom was delighted, and so they built the house and the nursery and the playground, just as exactly as they had planned.

And as far as I know, they are there still.